Ruthie
and the (Not So) Teeny Tiny Lie

Laura Rankin

BLOOMSBURY
CHILDREN'S
BOOKS

First published in Great Britain in 2008 by Bloomsbury Publishing Plc
36 Soho Square, London, W1D 3QY

First published in America in 2007 by Bloomsbury USA Children's Books
175 Fifth Avenue, New York, NY 10010

A CIP catalogue record of this book is available from the British Library

ISBN 978 0 7475 8745 3

Printed in China

1 3 5 7 9 10 8 6 4 2

All papers used by Bloomsbury Publishing are natural, recyclable products made from
wood grown in well-managed forests. The manufacturing processes conform to the
environmental regulations of the country of origin.

For all the wonderful teachers
who help our children through their
(not so) teeny tiny troubles

Ruthie loved tiny things — the tinier the better.
Her toys were the teeniest imaginable. She had dinky
dinosaurs, itty-bitty trains, ponies no bigger than your
pinkie and teddy bears that were barely there.

Ruthie loved finding tiny treasures too. At the beach she searched for the smallest seashells. The flowers she picked were no bigger than fairy wings. She even had an eggshell from a hummingbird.

And wherever Ruthie went, she carried
some teeny thing in her pocket.

One day at school breaktime, after skipping and playing
on the swings, Ruthie took a turn on the twirling bar.

When she landed, she saw something in the grass. It was a little box with a teensy window and an even tinier button on the top. She couldn't believe her luck. It was a teeny tiny camera.

Ruthie looked through its little window. Then she pressed the button on the top to take a picture. CLICK! Just like a real camera. This was absolutely the best thing Ruthie had ever found, and it was hers!

CLICK! CLICK! She had a great time trying it out.

"Say cheese, clouds." CLICK!

"Say cheese, little bug." CLICK!   "Say cheese, school." CLICK!

"Say cheese, Martin." CLICK!
But Martin didn't say "Cheese." Martin said,
"Hey, that's my camera!"

Ruthie was startled. "No it's not, it's mine."
"Give it to me," said Martin. "It's mine!"
"It is not!"
"Yes it IS."

"No it's NOT!" shouted Ruthie, and she raced back to class.

"What's going on?" asked Mrs Olsen.
"Ruthie's got MY camera!" cried Martin. "I got it
for my birthday and I dropped it in the playground."

But Ruthie wanted that teeny tiny camera in the worst way.
"It's mine!" she yelled. "I got it for MY birthday!"
Well, that wasn't true at all. Not one teeny tiny bit.

Mrs Olsen looked at Martin. She looked at Ruthie.
"Goodness, this *is* a problem," she said. "The camera can't
belong to both of you. I'll keep it safe in my desk drawer
for now. Let's talk about it again tomorrow."

Ruthie's stomach flip-flopped
during the rest of the day.

She couldn't remember
the answer to 2 + 2.

When Mrs Olsen read
a story, every word flew
straight out of the window.

The bus ride home took for ever.

"Hi, Ruthie," said Mummy. "How was school?"
"OK," mumbled Ruthie.

Dinner was macaroni cheese, Ruthie's favourite,
but she couldn't eat. Not one little bite.
"Aren't you feeling well?" asked Daddy.
"I'm not hungry," she said.

At bedtime, Ruthie was close to tears.

"What's the matter?" asked Mummy.

So Ruthie told Mummy and Daddy the whole story.

"What do you think went wrong?" asked Daddy.

"I said it was my camera," cried Ruthie, "but it's not!"

"It's going to be OK," said Daddy. "You made a mistake, and tomorrow you can sort it out. I think Mrs Olsen and Martin will understand."

But the next morning, Ruthie could barely eat. Maybe Mrs Olsen wouldn't understand. Maybe Ruthie would have to sit in the naughty corner. Maybe Martin would never talk to her again. Maybe *no one* would ever talk to her again . . . not one teeny weeny word.

The school bell was about to ring.
Ruthie took a deep breath and began
the long walk to the front of the room.
Mrs Olsen's desk seemed very far away.

"Good morning, Ruthie," said Mrs Olsen.
"I have something to tell you," said Ruthie in a very
small voice. "The camera isn't mine. I didn't get it for
my birthday. I found it in the playground."

Mrs Olsen didn't make her sit in the naughty corner. She didn't even look angry.

Instead, she gave Ruthie a hug and kissed the top of her head. "Thank you for telling the truth," said Mrs Olsen. "That took a lot of courage."

"I'm very sorry, Martin," said Ruthie.
"It's OK," said Martin.

All at once, Ruthie's stomach stopped flip-flopping. She even skipped a little on the way back to her desk.

She got the right answer to 3 + 7 in Maths.

After lunch, Mrs Olsen read the funniest story
Ruthie had ever heard.

And on the short bus ride home, Ruthie realised
that she didn't miss the teeny tiny camera . . . not
one teeny tiny bit.